Isobel C. Cholmeley

The Fountain and other Poems

SALZWASSER
VERLAG

Isobel C. Cholmeley

The Fountain and other Poems

Reprint of the original, first published in 1858.

1st Edition 2023 | ISBN: 978-3-37515-220-8

Verlag (Publisher): Salzwasser Verlag GmbH, Zeilweg 44, 60439 Frankfurt, Deutschland
Vertretungsberechtigt (Authorized to represent): E. Roepke, Zeilweg 44, 60439 Frankfurt, Deutschland
Druck (Print): Books on Demand GmbH, In de Tarpen 42, 22848 Norderstedt, Deutschland

THE FOUNTAIN,

AND OTHER POEMS.

THE FOUNTAIN,

AND OTHER POEMS.

BY

ISOBEL C. CHOLMELEY.

" What I write I cast upon the stream,
To swim or sink—I have had at least my dream."

BYRON.

———————————

LONDON:

CHARLES J. SKEET, PUBLISHER,

10, KING WILLIAM STREET,

CHARING CROSS.

1858.

DEDICATION.

———◆———

My own dear mother! when, long while ago,
   With falt'ring baby lips, thy name I breathed,
What lavish rain of kisses would o'erflow
   The little nestling face, that lay all wreathed
In thy bright-cluster'd ringlets—falling low!
   Ah happy memories! evermore bequeathed
From passing year to year; until the last
Shall vanish like the rest—and life itself be past.

Time has wrought many a change in thee and me.
   The soft dark tresses—silvered here and there,—
Are gathered smoothly back, no longer free
   To curl for pastime, round thy features fair:
The tiny child that babbled at thy knee
   Has grown to womanhood; and now must share
In all a woman's passions, hopes and pain:
Yet turns to thee—a child in heart again.

Turns, with a longing soul, from the sweet South
   To where her native cliffs rise white and grand :
Turns with a sigh to those fond days of youth.
   And though no warm clasps of that gentle hand,
No tone, no tender kiss from thy dear mouth,
   May greet the dreamer in the distant land.
The smile I may not see, will spring to hail
These first untutored lines—as once those accents
    frail.

Rome, April, 1858.

CONTENTS.

The Fountain

1.

In the palace garden there's a fountain,
Ever striving towards the clear blue heavens,
Ever dashed in diamond tear-drops downwards;
And the stately cypresses stand round it,
And each wears a golden crown at sunset,
Wears a regal crown of red gold sunshine;
And at sunset, in the palace garden
Sate the fair Rahämi, the king's daughter,
With her maidens and the minstrel Herah
And the noble guest, the dark prince Mirza.

2.

Rush of dancing feet and clash of cymbals
Oft had quelled the murmur of the fountain,
But at sunset all was hushed in silence,
Save the music of the gushing water,
Save the murmur of its ceaseless falling:
E'en the breeze swung languidly full freighted
With the rich rose odours and the jasmine
And a train of vague, voluptuous visions,
Fraught with irresistless influences,
Filled the heart, and held each sense in keeping.

3.

And the minstrel's eyes dwelt on the fountain,
And Prince Mirza looked upon the princess.
Gazed well pleased, like a sated lion;
But Rahämi raised her golden lashes,
Saying, " Wherefore sit we here in silence,
" While our guest keeps countless store of legends,
" Miserlike, and tales of flood and battle,
" Wherewith terrors past to present pleasure,
" He might change at will ?—and thou our Herah,
Has thy voice no song, thy lute no music ?"

4.

Then the fair court ladies smiled together,
Smiled to trace the heart's unquiet beating
Through the smooth-drawn web of silken phrases;
Smiled to see the red blood surging, swelling
Underneath the swarthy brows of Mirza;
But the minstrel Herah answered softly,
As one still half lost in dreamy musing,
" Princess ! I was grieving that the fountain,
" In its never-ceasing tearful striving,
" May not reach the beautiful blue heavens."

5.

And Rahämi heard the minstrel Herah,
Trembling like a harp touched by its master;
And glanced downward, while unwonted blushes,
Rushed o'er cheek and forehead, half eclipsing
The white glory of her maiden bosom;
Then looked up, and with a sudden motion
Banished from her brow the shading tresses,
Shook the liquid languor from her eyelids—
And her ladies marvelled; but Prince Mirza
Gazed on Herah, as once Cain on Abel.

6.

In the woods around the palace garden,
There's a din of hounds, a cry of horsemen,
For the stranger Mirza, with young Herah,
Rides at early morn to hunt the red-deer:
But Rahämi on her restless pillow,
Tosses, till the sun has drunk the dew-drops;
Then with murmurs, like a child half-weary,
While her tiny rose-lined feet, unslippered,
Kiss the roses on the broidered carpet,
Stretching her white arms, she calls her maidens.

7.

Through the forest by the palace garden
Rides Rahämi, underneath the shadows
Of the mossy-footed, wide-arched oak trees;
But the sweet unrest that stirred her slumbers,
Still through pulse and vein is thrilling, throbbing;
Shows in every deepened curve and colour
Of lips, softly swelling, scarcely parted,
(Crimson fruit grown ripe in southern sunshine)
In the careless flow of fragrant tresses,
Half dishevelled by her rapid going.

8.

Soon to charm away the fitful fever,
With its kisses came the cooling west wind;
Came from far foam-latticed sea-side grottoes,
Over crystal streamlets, fern-embowered,　　　[som,
Through the myrtle boughs, starred white with blos-
Down the long long aisles of the green forest,
Where the young Rahämi, the king's daughter,
Rode beneath the many formëd shadows,
Rode beneath the changing chequered shadows,
Of the mossy-footed, wide-arched oak trees.

9.

Hark ! a sudden shriek rang through the forest !
Down among the mosses in the thicket,
Kneels Rahämi, where the minstrel lieth,
Swathed in sleep—yet all too wan for sleeping :
Parts with trembling hands the golden tresses,
Sees the fair face, like a fading flower
With the death-dews freshly sprinkled o'er it;
Sees the ground all damp with Herah's heart's blood
While beneath the grass, like eyes of serpents,
Gleam the rubies of Prince Mirza's dagger.

10.

And she sinks beside him, wildly weeping,
And her virgin lips, all pale with anguish,
Faintly seek the death-pale lips of Herah :
Till the warmth of falling tears and kisses
Stirred the minstrel from his icy slumber :
Till the life spark feebly sprang and flickered
Underneath his closing violet eyelids ;
Till he murmured blissfully in dying,
" Lady I was dreaming that the fountain
" Touched with one bright leap the clear blue
      heavens."

Chastelard.

"D'une plainte incertaine,
De sanglots toute pleine
Je veux chanter
La misérable peine
Qui me fait lamenter."

CHASTELARD.

1.

Love led me from the summer shores of France
  To this bleak clime, (my prison-bars between
How drearily the rain-drops splash and dance).
  I was a simple knight, she Scotia's queen,
And yet I loved her for my dire mischance;
  I love her still, would God that she had been
The very poorest maid beneath the sun!
  Then had I worshipped thus, but not been thus
    undone.

2.

For days and months I never told my pain,
  Save to the wailing sea, and stars, and sky;
The wild winds swept away full many a strain,
  Wherein I mourned my ladye's cruelty,
And my youth's spring-time perishing in vain.
  That night, methought a brighter destiny
Dawned in her smiling eyes; she bade me bring
  My silver toned lute, and sit by her, and sing.

3.

T'was my whole heart that thrilled with each full
      chord;
  The fond, wild hope in silence held so long,
Sprang to my lips with every passionate word:
  And there were murmurs from the listening throng,
" Ah poet ! thy love-tears are fitly stored,"
  " Like pearls upon a golden chain of song."
But she leant o'er me, and I felt her press
  My hand, that trembled in that mute caress.

4.

And then she left me, all my being tost
  In a strange storm of joy, the while I strayed
From her sweet presence, through the crowd, and crost
  The dazzling halls; at last, in the dim shade
Of a dark corridor, my way was lost;
  But I passed onwards, where white radiance played
Through a half-open door, athwart the gloom,
  From lamps of alabaster.   Rich perfume

5.

Filled the lone chamber, and suffused the sense
  With a voluptuous charm of vague desire;
High rose the antique couch, by golden fence
  Closed in, and here were flow'rs, and there the lyre
She touched so well; one moment, in suspense
  I gazed, and then, my veins ran liquid fire,
For that I knew this was the balmy nest
  Where my bright bird of beauty sought her rest.

6.

Hark! there were voices—'neath the purple fall
  Of broidered arras, draping a recess
Where loured the dim grand windows, peaked and tall
  I hid me: soon, that sovereign loveliness
Came with her blythesome train; the secret thrall
  Of some unquiet thought, seemed to possess
Her gentle soul, half weary of their mirth;
  And sad, sweet eyes, that languid, sought the earth.

7.

I saw each shining jewel leave its hold,
  On veil and vest and sleeve, until thereby,
The regal garb dropt from her, fold by fold;
  And all that perfect form, dawned rosily,
Through white transparent clouds; the massy gold
  Scarce loosed, of her long tresses, with a sigh
She waved her maidens forth, as solitude,
  Were the best solace, for her pensive mood.

8.

All drooped she sate, with her red lips apart,
  Low murmuring fragments of my pleading strain,
The curtained arras trembled 'gainst my heart,
  In its wild throbs of mingled bliss and pain :
At last she breathed my name, with sudden start
  Raising her fair, flushed face, and wept, Oh then,
Grown mad with love, from that dark lair I burst,
  And clasped her in mine arms, to 'suage my
    passion's thirst.

9.

T'was but a moment, in the next, her eyes
  Struck through me, pierced me, glittering like cold
    steel,
Till I fell faint before her ; there were cries
  Of "treason !" "treason !" and I seemed to feel
The clutch of mailëd hands ; half vision-wise,
  Dark forms bent o'er me ; but my brain 'gan reel,
And all was blank, and then—I was alone,
  Chained like a felon to this dungeon stone.

10.

I die to-morrow ; I am dying now,
The headsman's axe but gives the mercy-stroke ;
To touch such heights of hope, then fall so low !
T'was little marvel that my heartstrings broke,
In those black depths of miserable woe.
Ah God ! t'was a wise word the poet spoke,
" Happy the dead who nothing more desires ;" *
Come then, keen death ! and quench these restless
fires.

---

* " Il marcha à l'échafaud en récitant 'l'épitre à la mort' de son ami,
Ronsard, dans laquelle se trouvaient ces vers ;—
    Le désir n'est rien que martire
    Content ne vit le désireux
    Et l'homme mort est bien heureux
    Heureux qui plus rien ne désire."
    Histoire de Marie Stuart. Par M. Mignet.

Last Night.

Last night the silver viols played,
And thousand lights gleamed down, and made
  An aureole in his golden hair.
I felt as I were borne along
By some archangel, swift and strong,
  In spheréd flight through rushing air.
    The day is past, the red sun set,
    Oh Time! glide faster, faster yet,
    And bring my lover here again.

We strayed out from the crowd alone,
On the carved balcony of stone,
    Carved quaintly like an ancient tomb;
And down below the nightingale
Sang in the moonlight calm and pale,
        Through tangled maze of jasmine bloom,
        Sang as I hear it singing now;
        Oh weary time so dull and slow!
        When will my love be here again?

Tracing the marble imagery,
Listing the warbled melody,
    Seeking perversely, far and near,
All, save that face, too fair, too·dear;
All, save the voice I pined to hear;
    I stood up in the moonlight clear.
        The bright young stars are in the sky;
        Oh weary time glide swiftly by!
        And bring my lover here again.

At last he spoke, I turned and looked
On him I loved, our passion brooked
   No crossing shadow of controul.
He knelt down lowly at my feet,
I felt his gaze, so keen, so sweet,
     Pierce through me to my very soul.
       Oh laggard time glide swiftly by,
       Life's golden sands drop lavishly !
       Till my dear lover come again.

And I grew faint, and could have died
Like a frail flower, that openeth wide
   Its longing heart to the searching sun,
To the tremulous rapture of love and light,
Till its crimson leaves wax wan and white,
     And it dies in the warmth it dotes upon
       Ah time glide swiftly swiftly by,
       Life's golden sands drops lavishly !
       Till my dear love is here again.

Ah softer far than song of bird
His upward look, the winning word
   That claimed me for his own, his wife;
I could not speak, but not in vain
Their pleading thrilled through heart and brain,
   I gave him all, my love, my life.
      Oh weary time glide swiftly by !
      No, no, stand still for ever and aye,
      For now my love is here again.

Earth's Lament.

Earth sat wailing and desolate, Earth the disconsolate
    mother
Crying aloud in her agony "Zeus! oh thou mighty
    and merciful,
Since my children, the strong and the beautiful, fade
    on my bosom,
Let me perish, me also; let thy lightnings consume
    me!

Out from my quivering heart sprang an oak
    wide-spreading and lordly;
Humbly the nations bowed down, mute and abashed
    at his presence,
See where he lies in the dust, withered and torn by
    the storm-wind.
Let me perish, me also; let thy lightnings consume
    me!

Mine was a rose-bud opening ripe to the amorous
    sunbeams
Bright as the blossoms Elysian, bound on the brow
    of thy Hebe,
Death the destroyer, the despot, plucked it with
    pitiless fingers—
Let me perish, me also; let thy lightnings consume
    me!

Mine was a lily of lilies, pure as the snows of
    Olympus;
Sorrow and Time came by; weary with Sin on their
    shoulders:
Stained and broken it fell, fell under their ponderous
    footsteps!
Let me perish, me also; now let thy lightnings
    consume me!
Earth sat wailing and desolate; Earth the disconsolate
    mother.

The Girl and the Roses.

SONNET.

In a churchyard's solemn shade,
 Grew a rose-tree, wan and frail;
 And its roses seemed to wail,
" Give us sunshine, or we fade."

Like the roses, drooping, pale,
 At her casement leant a maid,
" Love me or my life must fail,"
 Weeping low, the maiden said.

While she wept and watched again
 Came no friend to soothe and save,
  Death, not Love, stole softly near,

Laggard Love, that mourned in vain,
 Strewed the roses on her grave,
  In the sunshine bright and clear.

Sonnet.

" Non è minor il duol perchè altri il prema
Nè maggior per andarsi lamentando."
PETRARCA.

Keen pity and deep love, have struck me down;
At one fell blow, as of a two-edged sword;
And fain would bring me, bound with chain and cord,
To pay leal homage to thy beauty's crown:

Yet must I, rebel, with a darkling frown,
Vex the bright presence of my heart's dear lord;
Ape cruel calm, and lightly mocking word;
And my soul's secret longing still disown.

There stands a statue in the desert, free,
When matin rays fall on't to sigh and sing,
And blush with the red sunlight, humanly:

But I wait for the shade, in reverie
To give my passionate thoughts their swoop of wing,
When far from danger, as my Sun from me.

Alpha and Omega.

Oh Love! Oh Death! alike in this,
  That our best boons are of your giving;
Life's deepest draught of nectared bliss,
  And Lethë, when we're tired of living.

A Fragment.

They parted, never more to meet on earth:
　But once, as years rolled on, his child's fair face,
Lit the bleak darkness of his lonely hearth;
　Pale, beautiful, and pure from his disgrace,
As lilies, from the soil that gave them birth,
　Yet stamped with all the pride of his proud race.
He gazed on her, and wept; he dared not bless
That virgin fruit of his foul selfishness.

She passed—she left one kiss upon his lips,
  Of pardon, not of love, 'twas all she might;
For she had borne such agony, as strips
  Faith of its fervour, life of its delight:
Had seen the rush of conscious blood, eclipse
  Her mother's brow; then leave it damp and white.
While fell from one held sacred as God's name,
The broken story of her wrong and shame.

Ariella.

Where is she now
  That we loved so well,
With the lily brow,
  Oh who can tell?

Is she far away
  'Neath the waters fair,
Where the wavelets play
  With her wreathèd hair?

Or does she dwell
  In some Eden bower
Asleep in the bell
  Of its whitest flower?

In the hidden light
Of some ruby mine,
Does she rest, more bright
Than its gems can shine?

Where is she now
That we loved so well,
With the lily brow,
Oh who can tell?

Song.

The lakelet sleeps in the moonlight,
　The bird sleeps on the tree;
But I lie awake in the darkness,
　Awake, and thinking of thee.

I think, in the weary darkness,
  Of thine eyes blue, lustrous sheen,
Thy lips with their yesterday smiling,
  And their kisses—that have been.

The lakelet sleeps in the moonlight,
  The bird sleeps on the spray;
False love, on thy dreamless pillow,
  Sleep safe and softly as they.

Perdita.

They bid me look up, from my treasure of clay,
To the chrystalline sea, where the seraphim stand,
Where for me a new seraph prays softly to-day;
But the glory shines dimly, so far, and so high;
And I sit in the valley of shadows; and sigh
For the voice, and the lip, and the warm-pressing hand.

Let me dream—let me drink the full cup to the lees;
Till the poison of mem'ry burn deep in my breast,
O her bright laughing wiles ! who shall cheer me for
   these ?
And the frown, half in sport, when her brow's clear
   expanse
Was just stirred—as the wing of a swallow might
   glance
O'er a pure silver lakelet, scarce ruffling its rest,

Fair form that I worshipped ! fair face that I kiss,
For the last—the last time; and my tears flow alone,
And thy still, smiling beauty unmoved sleepeth on :
Fare thee well, fare the best, there's yet comfort in
   this,
Take the grave for thy home—mine the world without
   thee;
Go, lost love ! leave the darker and colder for me.

Absence.

WHEN the first matin beams
Stir thee from happy dreams,
          I think of thee ;

When the night breezes sigh,
Lovingly, tenderly,
          I think of thee.

Dull 'mid the festal throng,
Weary of smile and song,
       I pine for thee.

Lost in the forest's pride,
Lone by the altar's side,
       I pray for thee.

Thrilled by a lip that's gone,
Listing a voice far flown,
       I dream of thee:

Take pity love, and come,
Lest in the dearth and gloom
       I die for thee.

In the Morning.

My heart is heavy and weary,
  I dreamt a dream last night:
I would I had died, so dreaming,
  Before the morning light.

I dreamt I was loved and loving;
  I dreamt my lover was mine:
My head on his heart was resting,
  His hand was clasped in mine.
And soft through the wreathed lattice
  The summer breezes fine,
Strewed the loose-falling leaflets
  Of rose and jessamine.

My heart is heavy and weary,
My love and my lover are gone :
I wake, in the chill grey morning,
Alone—for ever alone.

From the German.

1.

Leaves and flow'rets gently tremble,
  In the cool, soft, evening air;
All is joy, and canst thou leave me
  Thus alone in my despair?
Stay with me, nor seek to roam,
In my heart is yet thy fairest home.

2.

I have loved thee without measure,
  Never wronged, through all the past,
And I feel thy dear hands' pressure,
  And thy tears fall warm and fast,
Weep no more, nor seek to roam,
In my heart is yet thy dearest home.

3.

Trust me, in yon bright world-desert
    Few have hearts like thine and mine,
And thou know'st, for thee, unmurm'ring,
    Life itself would I resign—
Stay with me, no farther roam,
In my heart is yet thy truest home.

From the Tuscan.

No, no, "fair Bianca," never say again;
   Call me unhappy Bianca, if you will,
My beauty is all perished, with the pain
   Of loving without hope—and loving still.

I throw a palm-leaf on the sea, it sinks!
   Another's lead floats gaily to the strand.
Why am I in this weary world? methinks
   Pure gold would turn to iron in my hand.

Ah well! one of these days you'll feel your loss,

    Beppo, if thus you leave me in the lurch;

You'll find me some fine morning, hands across,

    Laid out all white and cold in the dim church,

Then how you'll weep for me! how you'll lament,

'Tis ever so—when love and life are spent!

Mariamne.

Mariamne! my beloved,
  Mariamne! lost and true,
  Mariamne, that I slew,
For the cruel doubt unproved;
  I am lying at thy feet,
            But the heat
Of these bitter tears I shed,
Will not warm nor wake the dead.

Closed the bright eyes, wont to quaff
  All the sunny light around:
  And the tresses—that unbound,
To the music of thy laugh.
            Lightly prest
  The live marble of thy breast—
Fallen backward in a heap,
            Seem to sleep.

And the lip, that at my touch,
  Like a ruddy rosebud flushed,
  Lies beneath it, cold and hushed
In a whiteness overmuch;
  Never lily of the vale
          Half so pale!

Mariamne! that I slew
  For the cruel doubt unproved, ·
Mariamne! my beloved,
  · Mariamne! lost and true
Let me die, here at thy feet,
            Since the heat,
  Of these bitter tears I shed,
  Will not warm nor wake the dead!